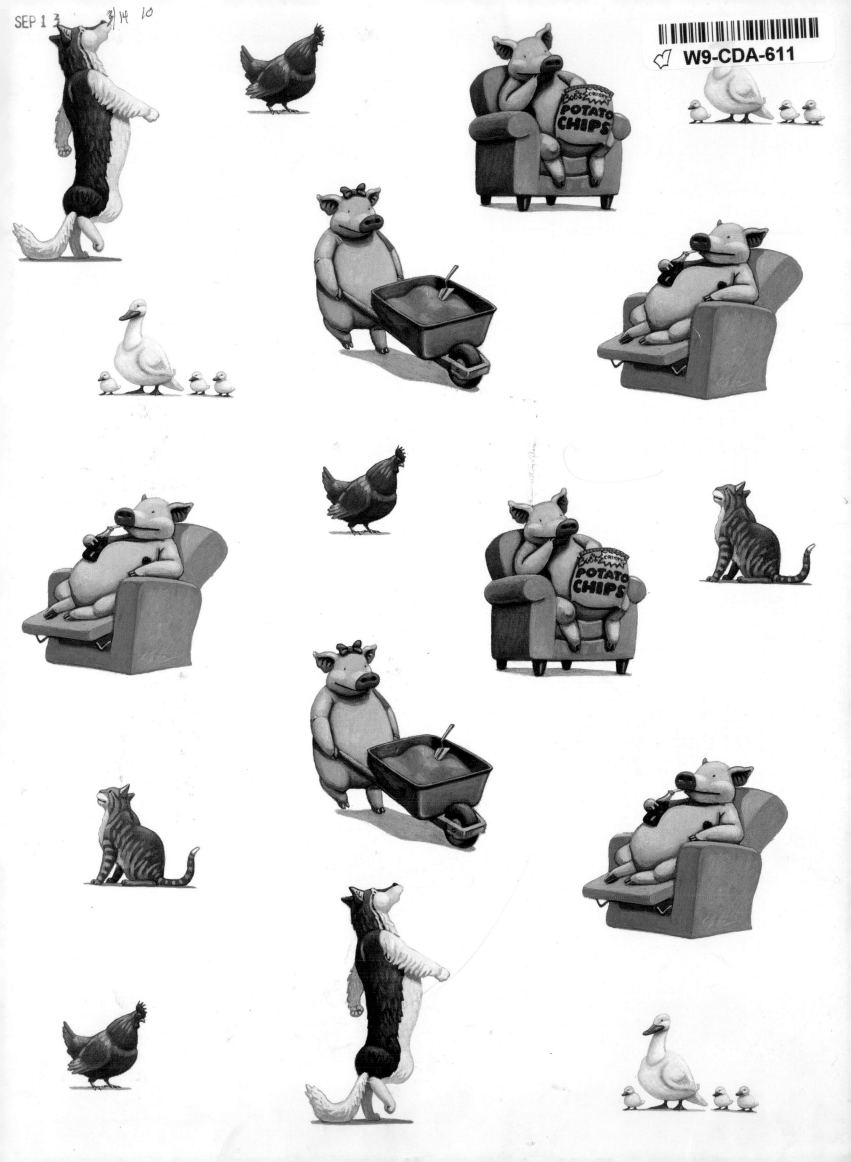

W9-CDA-611

THE THREE LITTLE PIGS

AND THE SOMEWHAT BAD WOLF

BY MARK TEAGUE

ORCHARD BOOKS · NEW YORK · AN IMPRINT OF SCHOLASTIC INC.

TO LILLIAS AND AVA: YOU HEARD IT FIRST

Copyright © 2013 by Mark Teague

All rights reserved. Published by Orchard Books, an imprint of Scholastic Inc., *Publishers since 1920.*
ORCHARD BOOKS and design are registered trademarks of Watts Publishing Group, Ltd., used under license.
SCHOLASTIC and associated logos are trademarks and/or registered trademarks of Scholastic Inc.

No part of this publication may be reproduced, stored in a retrieval system, or transmitted in any form or
by any means, electronic, mechanical, photocopying, recording, or otherwise, without written permission of
the publisher. For information regarding permission, write to Orchard Books, Scholastic Inc., Permissions
Department, 557 Broadway, New York, NY 10012.

Library of Congress Cataloging-in-Publication Data Available

ISBN 978-0-439-91501-4

10 9 8 7 6 5 4 3 2 1   13 14 15 16 17
Printed in Malaysia   108
First printing, May 2013

The display type was set in Circus Mouse Bold.
The text was set in Circus Mouse Book.
The illustrations are oil paintings.
Book design by David Saylor and Charles Kreloff

ONCE THERE WERE THREE LITTLE PIGS.
They lived on a farm, as most pigs do, and
were happy, as most pigs are. Then one day
the farmer told them that he and his wife were
moving to Florida. He paid the pigs for their
good work and sent them on their way.

"Let's buy potato chips," said the first pig.
"Let's buy sody-pop," said the second pig.
"Let's buy building supplies," said the
third pig, who was altogether un-pig-like.

Reluctantly, the others agreed. The first pig decided to build a straw house. Since straw is cheap, he had plenty of money left over for potato chips.

Bob's CRISPY!
POTA
C

The second pig decided to build a stick
house. Sticks are practically free, so he
had lots of money left over for sody-pop.

The third pig decided to build a brick house. She spent all her money on bricks and mortar, but the man at the hardware store gave her a sandwich.

Soon the straw house was finished. It was
dusty and musty, but the first pig did not mind.
He rocked in his hammock and ate potato chips.

Soon after that, the stick house was done. It was small and there was no room for a bathtub. But the second pig did not mind. He took a mud bath and drank sody-pop.

Brick by brick, the third pig worked on her
house. Sometimes the other pigs would come
by to watch. They had a wonderful time.

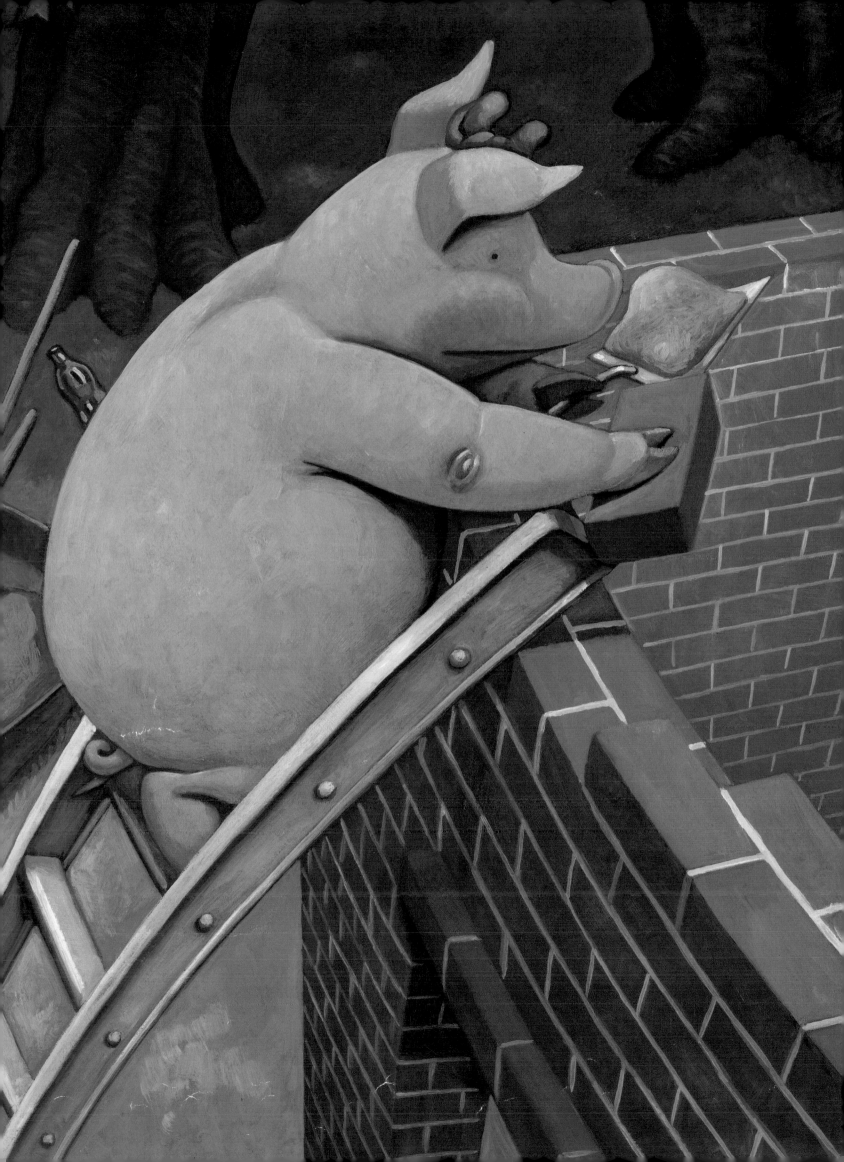

Finally, the brick house was finished. It was big, beautiful, and strong. The third pig was very happy. She filled a basket with vegetables from her garden.

The next day a wolf came to town. He was very hungry and somewhat bad.

He went to a donut shop, but it was closed.

He went to a hot dog stand, but it was locked.

Finally, he went to a pizza parlor, but he wasn't allowed in. He left in a **VERY** bad mood!

Soon he came to a straw house. It smelled like pig.
"I like pig," he said, not in a friendly way. He
banged on the door.
"Who is it?" called the first pig.
"The wolf. Open up, or I'll blow your house down!"
"I think the door is stuck," said the pig.
So the wolf HUFFED . . . And he PUFFED . . .
AND HE BLEW THE HOUSE DOWN!

"I can't believe that worked!" he said.
He had never blown down a house before.
Quickly, the first pig got on his scooter
and sped away.

The wolf moved on, hungry but confident. He came to another house, this one built of sticks.

"Same piggy smell," he said. He knocked on the door.

"Who is it?" called the second pig.

"Wolf. Open up, or I'll blow your house down! Trust me," he added, "I've done it before."

"I think the door is jammed," said the pig.

So the wolf took an enormous breath . . .

And he HUFFED . . . And he PUFFED . . .

AND HE BLEW THE HOUSE DOWN!

"I'm amazed that works," he said.
Meanwhile, pig number two got on his
bike and rode away. The wolf was still
hungry — VERY, VERY hungry.

The hungry wolf came to a beautiful brick house. He noticed a familiar scooter and bicycle, and the house reeked of pig. The somewhat bad wolf rang the doorbell.

"Who is it?" called the pigs.

"The WOLF! Open up, or I will blow this house down!"

"Oh, no," said the pigs. "Not now, we are watching our favorite show."

The starving wolf took a HUMONGOUS breath. And he HUFFED . . . And he PUFFED . . .

And he HUFF-HUFF-PUFFED AND PUFF-HUFF-HUFFED AND HUFFY-HUFFY-PUFF-HUFFED.

After the huffing and puffing stopped, the third pig said, "Do you think he is still out there?"

The three pigs looked through the window and saw the wolf collapsed on the lawn.

"Look at the poor guy," said the first pig. "He's exhausted. Maybe he needs some potato chips."

The second pig added, "And some sody-pop."

The three pigs revived the wolf with some smelling salts and invited him in. The somewhat bad wolf was embarrassed. "I was so hungry I could not think straight."

"Have a potato chip," said the first pig.

"Have a sody-pop," said the second pig.

"Never mind that stuff," said the third pig, "dinner is almost ready."

Since their houses were wrecked, the first two pigs moved in with the third pig.

"My house, my rules," she said. She made them clean their rooms before they went out to play.

The wolf stayed, too. But there was no more huffing and no more puffing. And he was hardly ever bad again.